# Little Bo Peep's Library Book

# CRESSIDA COWELL

*h*

*Hodder
Children's
Books*

Little Bo Peep had lost
her sheep and she didn't
know where to find them.

So Little Bo Peep went to the cornfield,
where she found . . .

. . . Little Boy Blue, reading a book.

'Is that a book about how to
find sheep?' asked Little Bo Peep.
'No,' said Little Boy Blue,
'but look in the library,
you might find one there.'

Basic
Bike
Horns

So Little Bo Peep went to the library,
where she found . . .

. . . Mother Goose,
the helpful librarian.

'Have you got a book
about how to find
sheep?' asked Little Bo Peep.
'I'm sure we have,' said Mother Goose.
'Lamb is in the cooking section,
you might find one in there . . .'

So Little Bo Peep went to the cooking section,
where she found . . .

pat-a-cake
pat-a-cake
BAKE
& ME

**Tarts**

Queen of Hearts

Basic Little Girl Cookery

Monsieur Loup

COOKING
WITH
FAT

Mrs A. Sprat

Cooking with Lean    Jack Sprat

Curd
and
Whe
Miss
Muf

Cooking

. . . the Big Bad Wolf, reading a book.

'Is that a book about how to find
sheep?' asked Little Bo Peep.

Basic
Little Girl
Cookery

Basic Little Girl Cookery

Monsieur Loup

Mons

**Basic Little Girl Cookery**

Monsieur Loup

*Basic Little Girl Cookery*

Monsieur Loup

BLACKBIRD & PIE

'Little Girl Cookery' contains 4 mouthwatering recipes from the kitchen of Monsieur Loup, the world-famous wolf chef. Monsieur Loup's previous book, 'Little Pig Cookery' was an international smash hit.

## Muffet & Blackbird Pie

SERVES 8

Ingredients

1 Little Miss Muffet
4 & 20 blackbirds
1 spider
10 oz pie pastry

Place all of the ingredients in a large bowl. Top with pie pastry and then bake in oven.

## Petite Fille avec Curl

SERVES 4

Ingredients

1 little girl with curl in middle of forehead
24 large truffles
4 oz butter
plenty of double cream.

For the more confident and experienced cook. Do something complicated with the truffles.

## Vegetarian Hotpot

SERVES 1

Ingredients

3 peas
1 piece of lettuce
salt & pepper
anything else you find in the fridge.

Important note: Little girls are notoriously difficult to catch. Put above ingredients on plate.

Mother Goose Library

Please return this book to
the library on or before the
last date stamped or fines
will be charged.

| 8 JUN 1981 | | |
|---|---|---|
| 5 OCT 1982 | | |
| 29 MAY 1985 | | |
| 5 APR 1989 | | |
| 10 JUL 1989 | | |
| 3 APR 1992 | | |
| 2 AUG 1997 | | |

PLEASE TAKE CARE OF THIS BOOK

This book is dedicated
to · Mum ·

Published by
Blackbird & Pie Ltd.
303, Sixpence Lane, Gooseville

Riding Hood Sandwich
SERVES 1

Ingredients

1 Little Red Riding Hood
1 seed bun
lettuce
ketchup

Toast both halves of the seed bun lightly.
Place little girl in between the 2 halves.

Also by the same author

Little Pig Cookery
by Monsieur Loup

Grandmother Cookery
by Monsieur Loup

Monsieur Loup lives all
alone in the dark woods.
He has no children.

'No sheep here,' said the
Big Bad Wolf, 'but thefts
are in the crime section,
you might find one there.'

So Little Bo Peep carried on looking.

And in the crime section she found . . .

. . . the Queen of Hearts, reading a book.

'Is that a book about how to find sheep?' asked Little Bo Peep.

Who stole the tarts?

Who stole the tarts?

*Who stole the tarts?*

Mrs A. Summer's-Day

This is another spine-tingling case for Detective 'Ace O' Heart. Can he track down the daring thief of **THE MISSING TARTS?**

Who stole the tarts of the Queen of Hearts? NOT Tom, Tom the piper's son, though he has stolen things before...

Who stole the tarts of the Queen of Hearts? The trail of jammy footprints leads straight to...

... the Knave of Hearts, who ate ALL those tarts, and now he doesn't feel very well.

ho stole
he tarts?

by
A. Summer's Day

Detective 'Ace'O'Heart is
quickly at the scene of
the crime... a trail of
jammy footprints could
be a vital clue.

gone

Who stole the tarts of the
Queen of Hearts? NOT little
Jack Horner who has eaten
enough already.

Mrs A Summer's Day's
thrilling crime novels
are loved by millions
across the globe.
She lives in a
little cottage in
the country with
her ten cats and
four and twenty
tame blackbirds.

This is a
Detective 'Ace'
O'Heart
book.

cover illustration
by Miss Muffet

'No sheep here,' said the
Queen of Hearts, 'but
animals are in the
natural history section,
you might find it there.'

So Little Bo Peep carried on looking.

And in the natural history section she found . . .

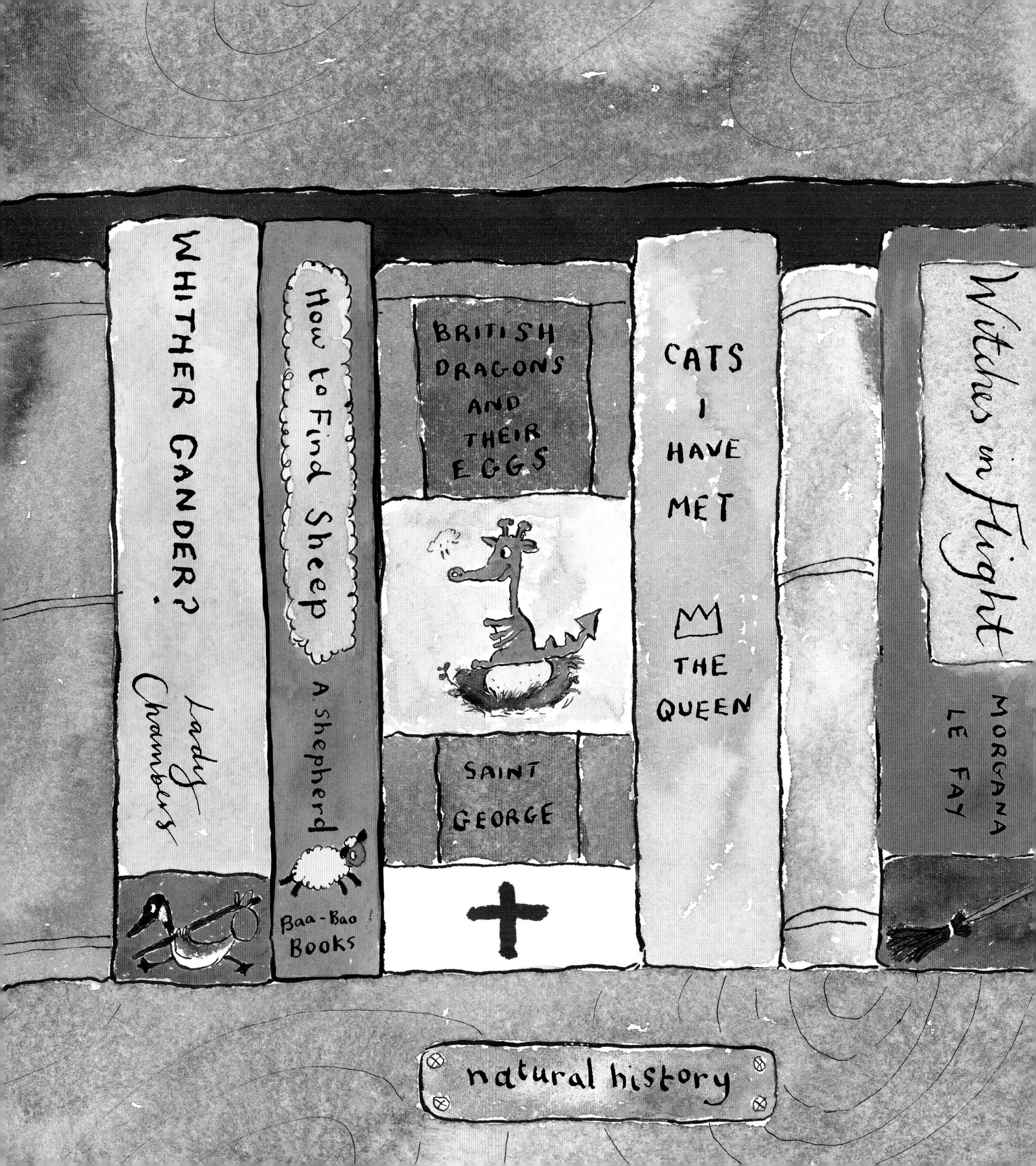

WHITHER GANDER?

*Lady Chambers*

How to Find Sheep

A Shepherd

Baa-Bao Books

BRITISH DRAGONS AND THEIR EGGS

SAINT GEORGE

CATS I HAVE MET

THE QUEEN

Witches in Flight

MORGANA LE FAY

natural history

tweet-tweet

. . . exactly the book she
was looking for!

How to
Find Sheep

by A. Shepherd

This book is dedicated to
anxious shepherds everywhere.
May they all find their she

Wagging their tails...    Behind them.

The End

How to Find Sheep

by A. Shepherd

Leave them alone...

And they will come home...

Look out for A Shepherd's next book, called "How to Find Ducks"

So Little Bo Peep borrowed that book from the library . . .

How to Find Sheep

by A. Shepherd

. . . and Little Bo Peep went home.

She sat down in her own front room and
she read that book again from cover to cover.

And when she had read it, Little Bo Peep went to her own front door and opened it, and looked outside where she found . . .

# SHEEP!

For Simon
C.C.

HODDER CHILDREN'S BOOKS

First published in Great Britain in 1999
by Hodder and Stoughton
This revised edition published in 2021

1 3 5 7 9 10 8 6 4 2

Text and illustrations © Cressida Cowell, 1999, 2021

A CIP catalogue record for this book
is available from the British Library.

ISBN 978 1 44496 499 8

Printed and bound in China

Hodder Children's Books
An imprint of
Hachette Children's Group
Part of Hodder and Stoughton
Carmelite House
50 Victoria Embankment
London, EC4Y 0DZ

An Hachette UK Company
www.hachette.co.uk

www.hachettechildrens.co.uk